12	DATE DUE	
2		
17		
MAR 2 88		
MAY 1 1		
13		

745
U

Urton, A.   c.1

50 NIFTY WAYS TO
MAKE MONEY

50 NIFTY WAYS TO EARN MONEY

Written by Andrea Urton
Illustrated by Neal Yamamoto

Lowell House
Juvenile
Los Angeles

Contemporary Books
Chicago

NOTE: The numbered piggy bank in the upper right-hand corner of each project indicates the level of difficulty; 1 being the easiest and 3 the hardest.

Publisher: Jack Artenstein
Editor-in-Chief: Lisa Melton
Director of Publishing Services: Mary D. Aarons
Project Editor: Amy Downing
Cover photograph: Tom Nelson

Library of Congress Catalog Card Number: 93-36833

ISBN: 1-56565-043-3

10 9 8 7 6 5 4 3 2 1

So, You Want to Earn Some Money?

Could you use a little extra cash now and then? Why not start your own business? The following section will show you how to get your business off the ground and have fun, too!

1. **Decide your goal.** Do you want an ongoing business, or are you considering a one-time project, such as a car wash or bake sale? Next, think about what you would *enjoy* doing. Do you like to spend time outdoors? Are you good with children or with animals? Are you artistic? Do you like to cook?

2. **Survey your neighborhood to get an idea of what services might be needed.** For example, if you live in a small town or in the suburbs, there may be a demand for lawn care or snow shoveling. If you live in a city, an errand or pet-walking service might be the perfect job. Be adaptable.

3. **Review your resources.** Before committing yourself to a project, ask yourself the following questions: Do I already have the materials or tools for the job, or will I need to invest some cash first? Do I have enough time? (Remember—homework comes first!) Do I have the skills or experience needed for the job? Do I want to work alone or with a partner (who will share the work and the profits)?

Costs and Fees

It isn't sensible to start a business unless you can make a profit. There are four main areas to consider when figuring out your costs and what you will charge customers.

• **Setup cost** is the money you spend to get started. For example, if you have a lawn-care service, you may need to buy tools. If you borrow money to start your business, that money must be paid back, so it is included in the setup costs.

• **Materials** are the items you need to perform your service or to make the product you want to sell. For example, if you have a bake sale, flour and sugar are two of the materials needed.

• **Labor** is the amount of time that you spend on the job. If you are decorating T-shirts, for example, you should include a fair price for your labor as part of the cost of the T-shirt.

• **Overhead** is the cost of running your business. It includes postage, advertising, and anything else other than tools or materials.

When working out a price or fee, first add up your costs, then decide how much you must charge to make a profit. The charts on the following pages will help you figure out how much to charge for your work. The three ways of charging fees can be used for the businesses in this book—just match one of the three corresponding symbols (a clock, a box, or an invoice) on the next two pages with the symbol featured with each project in the book. The following fees and costs are just examples. It is always helpful to find out what other people charge for the same job or product so you can be competitive.

Charging by the hour

Study Partner (found on page 36)

Setup costs:	none
Materials:	
notebook, pencil	$ 2
Labor:	
2 hours per week, at $3 per hour	$ 6
Overhead:	
bus fare: $ .75 each way twice a week	$ 3
TOTAL COST:	$11

$11 ÷ 2 hours = $5.50 per hour. This fee will cover your expenses and provide you with a payment of $3 per hour.

Charging by the product

Terrific Tees (found on page 64)

Setup costs:	
glue gun	$ 5
Materials:	
10 T-shirts, paint, sequins, glue	$ 35
Labor:	
2 hours per shirt, at $3 per hour	$ 60
Overhead:	
ad fliers (100)	$ 3
TOTAL COST:	$103

$103 ÷ 10 shirts = $ 10.30, the cost to make each shirt. Selling each shirt for $15 would give you a profit of $4.70 per shirt or $47 for all 10 shirts. If you continue your business, the cost to make each shirt will go down, because your setup costs have been covered. The next example shows you how you can spread costs and advertising over several jobs.

Charging by the job

To keep your prices at a reasonable level, you can spread your costs over several jobs. In this example we've added in 5 percent of these costs to each job. That means that the costs will be recovered once you have bathed 20 dogs (20 dogs x 5% = 100% of costs).

Puppy Parlor (found on page 34)

For 20 dogs	*Total costs*	*Cost per job* *(5% of total costs)*	
Setup costs:			
plastic tub, plastic leash, pet brush	$20	$1.00	
Materials:			
2 large bottles of pet shampoo (for 20 baths)	$10	$ .50	per bath
Labor:			
20 hours at $3 per hour	$60	$3.00	
Overhead:			
ad fliers (100)	$3	$ .15	
COST PER BATH		$4.65	

Your basic cost to give a bath is $4.65. If you charge $7.50 you will make a profit of $2.85 per job. You can also charge depending on how large the dog is. For example, you might charge an additional $1 or $2 for a dog with long hair that needs lots of brushing.

Your Business Kit

These items will be useful in any business that you choose:

- a customer file of names, addresses, and telephone numbers
- an appointment book or calendar
- a notebook to use to take notes when discussing a job with a new customer
- a notebook to keep track of income and expenses (see page 6)
- a receipt book (many clients will ask for a receipt for payment)
- business cards and/or fliers
- pen and pencil

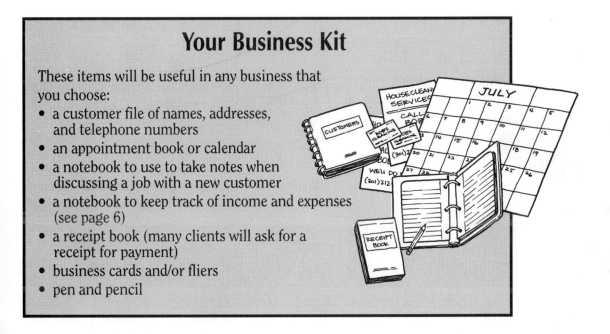

Keeping Records

To run a profitable business, you must be organized. Divide your notebook from your business kit into two sections: one for expenses (the money you spend) and one for income (the money you make). On each page of the expenses section, make four columns and give them the following headings:

EXPENSES			
DATE	ITEM	PURPOSE	AMOUNT

Whenever you spend money on your business, list the amount in the expenses section. Be sure to save all of your receipts, too.

On each page of the income section, make four columns and label them this way:

INCOME			
DATE	JOB/PRODUCT	AMOUNT	DATE OF PAYMENT

Before you begin your business, check with the chamber of commerce in your town to see whether you need any permits, or whether there are regulations you should know about. Also ask them about any tax laws that you must obey.

Saving

As you begin to see the extra cash flow in, it's important to put a portion of your income into a savings account.

First, decide on a reasonable amount to put away after each job or at the end of every month. You can save anywhere from 10 percent of your income to 100 percent! Then talk to your parents about which bank to use. There are many factors to consider, including how much interest you receive on your savings, how much you must pay for a finance charge, if any, and if you must keep a minimum amount in your account. You should also consider how close the bank is to your home and what the banking hours are.

Once you've decided on a bank, head over and tell the bank representative in "New Accounts" that you would like to open a savings account. You'll also receive a savings book to keep track of all your money. Have fun watching your savings account grow!

Get the Word Out!

Once you get a great business set up, there's one thing that's crucial to your success—customers! One way to attract customers is through advertising. Throughout this book you will find various advertising hints. Following are some advertising "basics."

Flier: A flier is a notice that you can put in a public place, such as a library, school, health club, grocery store, church, or synagogue. (Always ask permission from the business before you leave fliers.) The flier should describe your service or product and should let the customer know how to reach you. Colorful, creative fliers attract the most attention.

Business card: A business card is handy to leave with a customer. You can make your own cards from construction paper or from index cards cut into halves. Your card should include your business name, the type of job you do, your name, and your telephone number.

Word of mouth: A good recommendation from a happy customer is the best advertising. If you do a good job and are courteous and friendly, you may not even need to advertise.

Dealing with the Customer

If you are charging by the hour or by the job, you must get a clear idea of what your client wants done. Visit the premises beforehand and talk about the job with your customer. Always jot down any special instructions in a notebook. If you will be taking care of children or pets, this is the time to meet them.

Keep in mind that you have a responsibility to each of your customers. Be sure to do your work carefully and on time. If you are sick, give as much notice as possible, and try to find a friend to take over for you until you are ready to get back to work. If you are performing a service and are charging by the hour, be fair about how you use your time.

A Few Words About Safety

- Before you begin a new project, ask an adult to show you how to handle supplies and tools neatly and safely.
- When you meet a client for the first time, take along a friend. When passing out fliers to neighbors, do not go inside any house.
- Arrange for transportation to and from your job ahead of time.
- Always be sure an adult knows where you are, as well as when you will arrive at your job and the time you expect to leave. Always carry bus fare and change for a phone call.
- A new customer may interview you. Take this as an opportunity to interview the customer, too. You needn't work for anyone you are uncomfortable with.

Baking for Bucks

If you do not have the time to have an ongoing business, but you do want to raise money, a bake sale might be just the ticket. Holding such a sale can be especially profitable during holidays when people may stock up on home-baked goodies. This is a particularly good project to do with two or more friends.

What You'll Need

- business kit
- recipes
- measuring utensils
- food ingredients
- trays, platters, or large paper plates
- plastic food wrap
- brown paper bags
- long card table
- clean tablecloth
- $10 in change

Get Prepared!

To be successful, a bake sale needs to be advertised. Make plenty of fliers listing the location, time, and date of your event. Place the fliers on car windshields and on bulletin boards at markets in the immediate neighborhood.

Doing the Job

One week before:
1. If you are working with partners, have a meeting to decide which items, and how many, each person will prepare. You may decide to bake everything together. Some goodies that are popular at bake sales are pound cakes, cupcakes, turnovers, cookies, muffins, brownies, and fudge. It's best to work from recipes with which you are familiar.

The day before the sale:
2. Set aside several hours to get all the baking done. Begin by clearing your work space. Check to be sure that you have all your ingredients.

3. Read through each recipe once before you begin, and follow all of the instructions exactly. If you and your partners work together, one person can do the measuring and mixing, while another keeps the utensils washed.

4. Once the goodies are baked, give them plenty of time to cool, then frost cupcakes, cut brownies into 2-inch squares, and cut fudge into 1-inch squares. Arrange the items on trays so they can be displayed and sold individually. Cover each tray with plastic food wrap.

5. Before the end of the day, appoint someone to be in charge of taking the money and making change. That person is also responsible for bringing $10 in change to the bake sale, which will be reimbursed at the end of the day.

The day of the sale:
6. Set up a card table in the area where the sale is to be held. Cover it with a clean cloth, and set out the trays of baked goods. You'll probably sell more if you offer trays of small samples.

7. When a customer buys several items, pack them carefully in small paper bags. Don't forget to give them change, if necessary.

Going to the Dogs

What You'll Need

Most dogs love a chance to go for a nice, long walk every day, but many dog owners don't always have the time for this important task. If you like dogs, this is a good way to earn some money and to get fresh air and exercise as well!

- business kit
- sturdy walking shoes
- scooper and paper bag
- extra leash with a strong clasp
- dog biscuits (optional)
- small, coarse towel
- damp rag to wipe off the dog's feet

Get Prepared!

Note the homes in your neighborhood that have dogs in the yard, and leave a business card at each door. Leave business cards at veterinarians' offices, dog-obedience classes, and pet shops. Many apartment dwellers would also be happy to have their pets get extra exercise, so ask for permission to leave your cards or fliers in apartment lobbies.

Doing the Job

1. Be certain that the dog is secured on a leash before you leave the house. In good weather, a thirty-minute walk will generally be long enough. In very hot or cold weather, the walk should be shorter. Match your pace to the dog's. Young dogs will enjoy a brisk walk. Older dogs might prefer a slower pace.

2. Before crossing a street, have the dog sit at the curb. This will keep you from being dragged into the street by a huge dog and keep any bounding dogs from being run over. In a firm voice, use the dog's name and give the command to sit. You must be in control. If the dog doesn't obey, correct it with a quick, sharp tug on the leash. Never hit or slap a dog. Do not shout or give a command over and over. When it obeys, praise it.

3. Observe all laws regarding where the animal can relieve itself. Use your scooper and a paper bag to clean up afterward, and dispose of the bag properly.

4. When you return to the dog's home, be sure its feet are clean before it enters. If the owner has entrusted you with a key, check that the animal has fresh water and lock the door carefully when you leave.

Questions to Ask

Does the dog fight with other animals? What commands does it know? Is it afraid of traffic or other dogs? Is it okay to give the dog a treat?

THINK SAFETY! When you meet your walking partner for the first time, approach the dog calmly. Extend your open hand low, and with palm up, so the dog can see that you are not a threat. No matter how well behaved the dog or how protected the area, *always keep the animal on a leash.*

Party Time

What You'll Need

Get Prepared!

Doing the Job

Parties are fun, but they can be a lot of work, too. Grown-ups sometimes spend so much time taking care of details that they cannot enjoy their guests. A party helper's main job is to help the host or hostess wherever needed.

- business kit
- apron
- rubber gloves
- (formal party) a white blouse or shirt, and black pants or skirt
- (informal party) Ask the host or hostess what you should wear.

Prepare a list of services you provide, such as pre-party setup, food service, and cleanup. Put this list on a flier, make several copies, and deliver the fliers in person. Once you get started, ask your clients if they would mind if you set up an 8-by-10-inch card to advertise your service while you are working at their party. Then prospective clients will see how well you work!

1. Arrive at least an hour before the party begins so that you can help with any last-minute preparations.

2. If the host or hostess doesn't have a specific job for you at any given time during the party, clear away empty glasses and plates. Empty ashtrays when they are nearly full. Always be prepared with a dish towel to clean up spills as they happen.

3. For a buffet, be sure that food trays are filled and that napkins and utensils are available.

4. During the party, you may be asked to go out for supplies such as ice or extra soda. Put the cash that your client gives you in an envelope, and write the amount on the front. Return the change and receipt to your client.

5. If you wash the dishes as you go along, cleaning up won't be difficult. Spend an extra thirty minutes or so after the party to clear tables, finish up the dishes, and take out the trash.

Plants Need Love, Too!

What You'll Need

Get Prepared!

Doing the Job

When people go away on a trip, they enjoy themselves more if they know that things at home are being taken care of. Be a plant-sitter and give people peace of mind as you earn a paycheck!

- business kit
- plant book (or a contact person at a nursery who can give you advice if you need it)
- large key ring

Make up a flier (how about a leaf-shaped flier on green paper?) that outlines your services. You can care for indoor plants and water lawns, outdoor shrubs, and flowers, as well as bring in the newspaper and the mail.

1. If you are asked to bring in the newspapers and mail, or to turn on lights in the house to make it look occupied, you should visit at least every other day. To give the house a "lived-in" look, turn on a different light each time you visit.

2. To keep plants healthy and thriving, ask your client for a watering schedule and follow it. When you water, be sure that moisture doesn't seep through onto tabletops or carpets. Check the leaves at every visit for signs of any problems.

3. Keep your client's key on an oversized key ring so that you will not lose it. Double-check that all doors and windows are locked when you leave.

$$$ **TIP:** Although plants brighten up a waiting room or lobby, businesspeople are often too busy to care for them. If you find that plant minding is to your liking, you can expand your clientele to include offices or small businesses. Stop by each customer's business once or twice a week to water the plants, feed them when necessary, and clip away dead leaves.

Child Care

What You'll Need

A good baby-sitter will always find work and have a steady income. If you have younger brothers or sisters, you probably have much of the experience needed to care for children.

- business kit
- paper, markers, and other craft material
- snack (it's more professional to bring a snack instead of raiding the client's refrigerator)
- list of emergency numbers
- books

Get Prepared!

Baby-sitting is a big responsibility and must be taken very seriously. If you think this is the job for you, it is a good idea to take a baby-sitting course offered by the Red Cross or YMCA. Once you are ready, let neighbors with children know about your service. You will find that if you are pleasant and reliable, word of mouth will be enough to provide you with jobs.

Doing the Job

1. If you are sitting for a family for the first time, arrive at least thirty minutes early so you have time to ask questions and get instructions.

2. At first, the children may be a little nervous, but if you are calm and patient, you will win them over. Bring out the books and craft materials you brought from home. Children love playing with new toys and doing different activities. There are also plenty of crafts you can make with things around the house (masks from paper bags, for example), or games that you can play. They might also like to watch a video or tell stories.

3. Keep an eye on the clock, and have the children prepare for bed on time. Once they are in bed, check on them often. You can do homework or watch TV while they sleep, but remember that the children are your first responsibility.

THINK SAFETY! Keep all doors locked, and never let strangers into the home while you are baby-sitting. When the telephone rings, answer politely, but never tell anyone that you are the baby-sitter or that you are alone. Simply say that the homeowners are not able to come to the phone, then take a message.

Questions to Ask

What's the name and number of the family doctor? The number of a neighbor or relative to call in case of an emergency? The number where the parents can be reached? Does a meal need to be prepared for the children? Can the kids have liquids before bedtime? What is their bedtime?

From the Ground Up

What You'll Need

Get Prepared!

Doing the Job

The first lawn mower was patented in England in 1830, and it probably wasn't very long before some youngster realized that mowing a neighbor's lawn was a great way to make cash!

- business kit
- sturdy gloves
- rake
- broom
- trimming shears

On a business card or flier, indicate that the homeowner needs to provide the lawn mower or edger. Distribute the cards around your neighborhood, looking for lawns that need work.

1. This is a chore best done during the cooler hours of morning or late afternoon. If you are using a gas-powered mower, be sure that the tank is filled. If you add any gas, be sure to refuel in an open, well-ventilated area. Your client should supply the gas.

2. Before you begin, ask the client if the adjustable height setting on the mower is correct. If it's not, set it to the desired height. Remove stones, sticks, and other objects from the lawn.

3. Mow the lawn in a back-and-forth pattern. If the grass is long, mow in strips a few inches wide to prevent the lawn mower from overworking. If you are using a mower with a collector bag, empty the clippings wherever the client prefers. (*Always* turn the mower off before removing grass.) You may need to empty the clippings collector several times, depending on the size of the lawn. If the mower does not have a collector, you'll need to rake the lawn when you are finished mowing.

4. Use trimming shears to neaten around flower beds, driveways, and walkways. Clean and sweep driveways and walkways.

$$$ TIP: Don't quote a fee until you see the size of the yard.

Hoe, Hoe, Hoe

What You'll Need

In springtime, home gardeners often need a little help turning the soil and preparing their gardens for the growing season. If you have a green thumb, this may be the job for you.

- business kit
- sturdy gloves
- a book that describes garden flowers and vegetables, and identifies problem weeds
- hoe
- rake
- shovel
- hand trowel

Get Prepared!

Put together a list of the garden services you will offer—for example, tilling the soil (which means breaking up the soil and preparing it for planting), weeding, and planting seeds. Put this list in your fliers, and distribute the fliers to neighbors in early spring.

Doing the Job

1. If you will be tilling the soil, check a day ahead of time to see how firm it is. If the ground is hard, it is best to water it well the day before the job.

2. Remove all the weeds from the area, pulling out the roots whenever possible. (Be sure you know what your client considers a weed!)

3. Now you are ready to till the soil. First, lightly break up the ground with a hoe, then use a small shovel to dig down and turn the soil to a depth of 3 to 6 inches. You may want to use a hand trowel for small spaces.

4. Use your hoe once more to break up any large clumps of dirt, then smooth over the entire area with a stiff rake.

5. If you are planting seeds, now is the time to do it. Plant and water the seeds according to the package instructions.

6. Dispose of the weeds in the trash, then sweep the walkways and the driveways. Since weeding can be an ongoing job, ask your client if he or she would like to set up a summer schedule with you to weed the garden every two or three weeks.

Special Delivery

What You'll Need

Do you always get things done on time? Do you have a good memory for details? Are you well organized? If you answered yes to these questions, consider earning cash by providing an errand service for your friends and neighbors.

- business kit
- backpack
- fanny pack
- local map (optional)

(This list will vary depending on the transportation you are using. If you are riding a bicycle, add baskets or saddlebags. If you are taking the bus, carry plenty of change for your fare. If you are walking, use a cart or wagon of some sort.)

Get Prepared!

Check the businesses or services that are found in your area, such as the post office, grocery store, bakery, dry cleaners, pharmacy, bookstore, shoe repair, and other service-related businesses. On a flier, list all of the businesses that your errand service will cover, and distribute the fliers throughout your neighborhood.

Doing the Job

1. First, visit your client and bring along your notebook. If you are to drop something off (dry cleaning, for example), note the store name and address in your notebook. List the items, write down any instructions, and read them back to your client (i.e., "four white shirts, no starch, must have by Monday").

2. When you drop items off at a business, get a receipt and return it to your customer. Be sure to let the customer know when the items should be picked up, or if your schedule allows, work it out with the customer to pick them up yourself.

3. If you are picking something up, write the address and instructions in your notebook. If there will be a charge for the item, collect the money from your client, put it in an envelope, and mark the amount on the front. Keep the envelope safe in an inside jacket pocket or in a fanny pack.

4. When you make the payment, count your change on the spot to be sure it is correct. Do the errand and return immediately, then mark your time in your notebook. If you are stopping at several places, be sure to pack everything safely, and don't try to carry more than you can easily handle.

5. As you complete an errand, check it off your list. A forgotten item or something that has been done incorrectly will have to be taken care of at your expense. Double-check your list, and deliver any receipts or change.

$$$ TIP: To make the most of your time, you may want to schedule going to certain places on certain days. For instance, you may want to pick up your clients' dry cleaning on Mondays, go to the post office on Tuesdays and Fridays, and visit the shoe repair store on Wednesdays. Be sure that all your clients know your schedule.

Pet Pal

Most people consider their pets a part of the family, but a pet must often stay behind when the family goes away for a vacation. If you like animals, pet-sitting may be a good money-maker for you.

What You'll Need

- business kit
- large key ring

Get Prepared!

Make up a flier that outlines your services, then distribute fliers to dog owners at the local park. If you can get permission, leave fliers at veterinarians' offices, dog-obedience classes, pet shops, and pet-grooming salons.

Doing the Job

1. When caring for birds, reptiles, or fish, you may need to stop by only every other day. An apartment-bound dog, however, will require your attention at least twice daily. Spend about an hour at each visit, including some time playing with the dog or cat. Always be careful when entering and leaving the premises. A nervous dog or cat might try to get past you and run outside.

2. First, check that the pet appears healthy and alert. Be sure that there is plenty of fresh water, and keep the bowls and food area clean. If your charge is a cat, be sure that the litter container is clean. If your charge is a bird, reptile, or small mammal, fill the food and water containers, and clean the cage when necessary. When taking care of fish, don't clean the aquarium unless the owner has shown you exactly how.

3. Keep your client's key on an oversized key ring so that you will not lose it. Always double-check that all doors and windows are locked when you leave.

House Helper

What You'll Need

Few people enjoy housework. Many would happily pay for regular assistance with their chores or for extra help when they are particularly busy.

- business kit
- large plastic bucket
- rubber gloves
- vacuum
- glass cleaner
- scouring powder (nonscratching)
- furniture polish
- paper towels
- clean rags

(other tools you may find handy: soft bristle brush, two or three small sponges, mop, broom)

Get Prepared!

Likely customers for this service are senior citizens and families in which both parents work or in which there is a new baby. Put up fliers at markets, senior citizen centers, and churches or synagogues.

Doing the Job

1. Know the products you are using. Read all warning labels and follow them exactly! If there is anything you have a question about or a direction you don't understand, ask a parent to explain.

2. Everyone has his or her own method of doing household chores, but one rule that works well is to clean upper surfaces first, then clean the floors and carpets.

3. When dusting, carefully move small objects from tables and countertops, then replace them in exactly the same spots after you've dusted. After cleaning mirrors and glass, buff with a soft rag to remove streaks. Use a nonscratching cleaner to scrub tubs or sinks.

4. Before you vacuum the floor, check that the bag is not too full. Then, empty all trash containers.

5. Leave a small bouquet of daisies in the living room for first-time clients. This will leave a good impression. Still, there is no better advertising than a job well done!

Toy Haven

What You'll Need

PARENTAL SUPERVISION RECOMMENDED

The best-loved toys often suffer from too much attention. Dolls become dirty, and teddy bears may be ripped from too many hugs. If you are skillful, you can set up your own repair shop to revive those special toys.

- business kit
- needles
- thread
- ribbon
- hairbrush or comb

- mild soap
- washing machine and clothes dryer
- iron
- old pillowcase

(other tools you may find handy: enamel paint, brushes, clean rags or shredded fabric, scissors, wood glue, string, wire)

Get Prepared!

Colorful fliers are the best way to advertise this business. List the services you will offer, such as repainting doll furniture, repairing kites, gluing plastic toys, or mending doll clothes. Post the fliers at markets, at churches or synagogues, and (if you can get permission) at day-care centers.

Doing the Job

Since you will keep the toy while you repair it, give your customer a receipt on which you have written the customer's name, a description of the toy, an estimate of the cost, and the date when the job will be ready. Enter the same information in your notebook, along with the customer's address and telephone number. Label the toy and store it in a safe place.

There are many toy-repair services you could offer. Here are a couple of ideas:

Costume conditioning

1. Just as your clothes need to be taken care of, a doll's clothes need attention, too. Begin by repairing any rips or tears, then replace missing buttons or bows.

2. Hand wash the clothes in cool water and mild soap. Be sure not to mix clothes of different colors together because the dyes could run.

3. Hang the clothes to dry. When the fabric is just slightly damp, carefully press it with a warm iron. Get a parent to help you.

Bear repair

1. Most teddy bears don't mind a swim in the washing machine, but check to see what the bear is stuffed with first. If it is stuffed with foam rubber, set the machine on a more delicate setting than you would if it is stuffed with cotton strips. An adult can help you determine which washing machine setting is most appropriate.

2. Be sure the eyes and nose are on securely, and close rips temporarily with safety pins. If you have an old pillowcase, cut several small holes in it and place the bear inside for washing. That way, if an eye, nose, or some stuffing happens to work loose, it will be easier to find.

3. Wash the bear in mild soap on the gentle cycle. Use a clothes dryer to tumble the bear dry on a low, delicate setting. When your patient is clean, use shredded fabric as extra stuffing, if needed, to restore the bear to its chubby self.

4. Sew any rips closed. If the eyes or nose are missing, you can replace them by sewing on large shiny buttons or gluing on small circles of felt. Top off your fixed-up teddy with a bright red bow around its neck.

Sale of the Century!

A garage sale is a good way to turn items that you no longer need into cash. But if you don't have enough things for your own garage sale, don't give up. Try organizing and running a sale for friends and neighbors. You'll make money and help someone at the same time!

What You'll Need

- business kit
- three to five pieces of large, stiff cardboard
- colorful markers
- 3-by-5-inch notecards
- scissors
- tape
- straight pins
- stick-on labels or masking tape
- notebook
- pen or pencil

Get Prepared!

Begin by deciding what your service will include. For example, you might advertise the sale, arrange and price the items, assist your client during the sale, and clean up afterward. List these services on fliers and post them at local markets.

Doing the Job

The day before the sale:

1. Visit your client for an hour or so to help in pricing the items. Wherever possible, use stick-on price labels or masking tape. If a label won't stick (on clothes, for example), cut a 3-by-5-inch card in half, print the price clearly, and pin it to the item.

2. On several pieces of cardboard, use markers to write the words "GARAGE SALE TODAY!" in large letters, with the address and the time of the sale below.

The day of the sale:

3. At least 1½ hours before the sale, tape the signs you made to telephone poles at intersections near the sale.

4. Arrive at your client's home at least an hour before the sale so that you will have plenty of time to set up. Leave room between large items, such as furniture, so that customers can move around easily. Display small or fragile pieces as agreed upon with the client.

5. Once the garage sale begins, record each item sold in your notebook. Write a brief description of the item and its price. No matter how busy you are, take the time to count carefully the money you receive and to make the proper change. If you are in charge, place the money in an envelope or box that you keep with you at ALL times.

6. When the last customer has gone and all unsold items have been stored away, sit down with your client and settle the cash. With a calculator, add up the amount in your notebook, then make sure it tallies with the amount of cash in your envelope. After subtracting the amount of change you started with, your figures should be equal.

Questions to Ask

How will the items be displayed (on tables the client provides, or on sheets spread on the ground)? Who will be responsible for collecting money at the sale? Who is responsible for getting change for the sale (at least ten $1 bills and $5 in quarters)? What is the policy on checks? Is it all right to bargain with the customers?

 # The Traveling Lemonade Stand

What You'll Need

For decades the lemonade stand has been a part of summer life. By putting your stand on wheels you can give this old standard a new twist and earn some cold cash.

- business kit
- a store-bought lemonade mix or several lemons, sugar, and water
- one-gallon plastic jugs
- funnel
- measuring cup
- measuring spoons
- cooler or bucket with ice
- paper cups
- a wagon
- card table
- towel or clean tablecloth
- bag for disposing used cups
- $2 or $3 in coins for making change
- cardboard
- markers
- fanny pack

Get Prepared!

Scout out the area where you plan to set up your stand. You'll do best to begin on a busy street corner or near a park or playground. Once you've quenched everyone's thirst in one spot, use your cart or wagon to move your stand elsewhere—for example, to where people are doing yard work or holding a garage sale.

Doing the Job

1. On a large piece of cardboard, use markers to make a sign for your stand.

2. Before preparing your lemonade, wash your hands well. Clean the plastic jugs in hot, soapy water, then rinse them carefully.

3. You can make lemonade from a mix or squeeze your own. If you decide to make your own, experiment to find the recipe that you prefer. Begin by squeezing a cup of lemon juice and pouring it into a jug. Using a funnel, fill the jug with about 6 cups of cold water, then add 1 cup of water at a time. After each addition, pour a little into a glass and taste it, until you feel the mixture is right. Add sugar to taste 1 teaspoon at a time, then stir or shake. When you find the combination you like, write it down so you can make it the same way each time.

4. At your chosen location, set up your stand and place the sign where it is easy to see. Be sure to bring along your fanny pack with change.

5. When someone requests a cup of lemonade, take the cash and make change if you need to, then pour the customer a cup of lemonade. Don't fill the cup right to the top, or it might spill.

6. When you are ready to move on to another area, check to see that no paper cups have been left on the ground.

Something More

For variation, you could offer limeade or orangeade. Try mixing the juice with sparkling water or club soda. You can also give your customers a wider choice by offering a low-calorie alternative.

Beautiful Balloons

What You'll Need

Get Prepared!

Doing the Job

If you are imaginative, decorating with balloons for parties and holidays can be lots of fun, as well as a good way to earn extra income.

- business kit
- balloons
- tape

- string
- ribbon
- paper streamers

- access to a helium machine (optional)

Blow up some large balloons and, with a permanent marker, put your business name, phone number, and any other important information on each of them. Stick these balloons in such visible areas as churches, synagogues, and supermarkets. (Be sure to ask permission before putting anything up.)

Several days before:

1. Visit the place that is to be decorated, and make a list of the supplies you'll need. Ask your clients for a deposit that will cover your supplies, and give the clients a receipt for the deposit. Discuss with the clients what you plan to do, and give them an opportunity to add suggestions.

2. Purchase your supplies several days before the party. Be sure to pick up a few extra balloons.

The day of the event:

3. Arrive at least two hours before the event. This will give you plenty of time to blow up regular balloons and to decorate with streamers. Balloons can be tied to banisters or furniture with ribbons. If you are taping them in place, use masking tape, which can be easily removed later without leaving a mark.

4. You can group a few balloons together and use them as table centerpieces. Or, if you have access to a helium machine, fill the balloons with helium. Then, tie colorful ribbons around the knot of each balloon, and let the balloons float to the ceiling. The hosts and guests are sure to love any creative twist you give to the balloons!

Equipment Manager

Do you like team sports, such as baseball, football, soccer, or ice hockey? Being an equipment manager is a good way to earn extra cash when you aren't on the field yourself. The job involves passing out equipment and keeping track of it. A good equipment manager doesn't have to know everything about the sport, but you should pay close attention and learn as much as you can.

What You'll Need

- business kit
- soft rag

Get Prepared!

To find out who has a need for an equipment manager in your area, check with the coaches of local sports teams to learn their policies regarding equipment managers. Try Little League teams, the YMCA and YWCA, and city recreation departments. Some large corporations may also have employee softball teams.

Doing the Job

1. Before a game (take, for instance, baseball), be sure that you have all the equipment that will be needed, such as bats, gloves, balls, safety helmets, and masks. Check to see that everything is in good shape, and make a list of what you have. If you have to travel to the game site, be sure that all of the equipment makes it into the car, bus, or van.

2. Check that every player's uniform is complete.

3. During the game, keep an eye on the equipment, and use a soft rag to clean off anything that gets dirty. If something gets damaged or broken, set it aside for repair or replacement.

4. When the game is over, gather up all the equipment, and check it against your list. If anything has been damaged or is missing, let the coach know. Be sure that everything is put away safely in the equipment room or locker.

News and Views

A monthly newsletter can be a great opportunity for a junior reporter to keep the neighborhood up to date on local events.

What You'll Need

- typewriter or computer
- glue stick
- pens
- pencils
- notebooks
- several 11-by-17-inch sheets of white paper

Get Prepared!

There are two ways to earn money with a newsletter—selling issues and selling advertising space. In both cases, the best way to get customers is to print up a free sample issue that you can give to neighbors, friends, and local business owners.

Doing the Job

1. First, decide what will be in your newsletter. You could include book reviews, cartoons, short stories, poems, a puzzle or riddle section, a classified section, a sports section listing scores of local games, and a "new neighbor" section.

2. Allow at least two or three weeks to gather the material you've decided to include in your newsletter. If your friends offer to help, set a deadline for incoming material that gives you time to put the newsletter together and deliver it on time!

3. Carefully check all your facts. Triple-check names, dates, and addresses. Type your material in columns about $3\frac{1}{2}$ inches wide. Proofread the material for errors. (You may want to have a parent or teacher help with this.)

4. Now you will need to do what is called pasting up your newsletter. Start with a large sheet of paper (11 inches by 17 inches), with the 17-inch side along the bottom. Fold this in half. Each side of each half will be one page, giving you four pages total. Once you've done the newsletter a few times, you may want to add a sheet, making it eight pages long. Just remember, the bigger the issue, the more time and money it will take to put it out.

5. Cut out the typed columns and arrange them on each page so that they are easy to read. Leave spaces to paste in artwork or hand-lettered titles to give the newsletter a lively appearance. If the material doesn't fit, you may have to shorten a few stories or even cut a story.

6. Glue the segments down, including the art, the name of the newsletter (newspapers call it the masthead), the price, and anything else to complete your newsletter. The finished work is called a dummy.

7. Take the dummy to a copy shop and make as many copies as you need. If you copy the newsletter onto 11-by-17-inch paper, you can just fold it and deliver it. If you must copy the newsletter onto $8\frac{1}{2}$-by-11-inch paper, you'll need to staple the pages together.

8. Deliver your newsletter to each customer, collect payment, and let them know when they can expect the next edition!

$$$ TIP: The easiest way to charge for a newsletter is with a set price per issue. You can make more money, though, if you offer advertising space to businesses for a flat fee per issue. For example, for an ad that is about 2 square inches, you could charge $5 per issue. (You do need to limit the amount of advertising; otherwise, the paper will be boring.)

Car Care

What You'll Need

Few people want to take the time to wash the family car, so why not provide a house-to-house car-washing service as a business?

- business kit
- bucket
- soft rags
- mild soap (a little dishwashing soap works well)

- sponge
- soft brush
- glass cleaner

- paper towels
- hose with an adjustable nozzle

Get Prepared!

Fliers or business cards are the best way to let neighbors know you will be washing cars in their neighborhood. Be sure to tell them that your service provides all its own supplies, except for water. This is a great project for a few friends to do together.

Doing the Job

1. Begin knocking on doors and telling people about your service. Agree on the price before you start. Don't be disappointed if you are turned down—it happens to the best salespeople!

2. Once you find a customer, fill the bucket about ¾ full with soapy water. Use the hose to spray the entire car, then turn off the hose at the nozzle so that you don't waste water. Use a soft sponge to soap down and clean a small section of the car. Rinse immediately, and move on to the next section.

3. When cleaning the chrome or body of the car, use only soft cloths or sponges in order to avoid scratches. To clean the tires and headlights, however, you can use a very soft brush to remove stubborn dirt.

4. When you have washed the entire car, give it one final rinse with clean water. Dry the car completely with soft rags.

5. Use glass cleaner to clean the windows and mirrors inside and out. Wipe the dashboard and seats with a dry cloth. Sweep out the floor with a small brush. Empty the ashtrays. When the job is done, put a business card under the windshield wiper to let the customer know how he or she can reach you and when you'll be back in the neighborhood. When you get home, rinse out your rags and sponges.

Caddy for Cash

What You'll Need

Get Prepared!

Doing the Job

If you like spending time outdoors, being a golf caddy might be ideal for you. As a caddy, your main job is to carry the golfer's clubs and to keep your eye on the ball, but there are a few other ways that you might help your client.

- business kit
- soft rag

Check with golf courses in your area to learn their policies regarding caddies, especially their payment policies. Some courses hire the caddies, while other courses rely on the golfers to pay for their own caddies. Dress neatly and be courteous at all times.

1. A good caddy doesn't have to know everything about the game of golf, but he or she should be familiar with the course. One way to learn the course is to assist another caddy a few times for free. Get to know where the hazards, such as sand traps, are. Also note what is par (an acceptable number of strokes for an accomplished golfer) for each hole.

2. When you accompany your own client, use a soft rag to gently wipe off the clubs and ball as needed during play.

3. Keep as quiet as possible at all times. Don't offer help on how to approach a difficult hole, unless the golfer asks you.

4. Some clients will ask you to keep score. You can learn this from the golf pro or the manager of the course.

5. When the game is over, you can offer to carry the clubs to the golfer's car. Give your client a card so he or she can ask for you next time.

Puppy Parlor

If you like dogs and handle them well, bathing pets may be the job for you. You can also offer it as an extra service if you have a dog-walking or pet-sitting business.

What You'll Need

- business kit
- plastic measuring cup
- mild pet soap
- washcloth
- large plastic tub (for outdoor bathing)
- hose with an adjustable nozzle
- two or three dry towels
- plastic leash
- pet brush

Get Prepared!

Let neighbors know about your service. Take your business cards to the local park and pass them out to dog owners. If you can get permission, leave business cards at veterinarians' offices, dog-obedience classes, and pet shops. Pet bathing takes patience and practice. Start by bathing the family pet or a friend's dog until you are at ease with the job. Before beginning the job, check with the owners to see if they prefer whether you wash their dog inside or outside the house. (Usually, it's easier to wash a small dog inside; a large dog can be easily handled outside, in a fenced-in yard.)

Doing the Job

Inside:

1. Fill the bathroom tub with about 3 inches of water. Be sure that the water is at a comfortable temperature (from tepid to cool).

2. Remove the dog's collar. Place the dog carefully in the water. Speak to the animal and stroke it to keep it calm.

3. Use a plastic cup to wet the animal's coat, then soap it according to the package directions. Scrub gently with your fingertips. Don't get soap in the animal's eyes or ears. Use a damp washcloth to gently clean its face. If something seems to make the dog nervous, don't insist. If the animal is comfortable with you, your job will be easier.

4. Rinse the soap away as much as possible with the cup. Any soap left behind will make the dog itchy.

5. Drain the water from the tub and close the shower curtain or door so the animal can shake without getting the whole room wet.

6. Dry the animal with a towel. Follow up with another dry towel. Gently brush through the coat of a long-haired dog to remove tangles. You may want to finish with a pretty ribbon tied to the animal's collar. Keep the dog on a leash until the owner arrives.

Outside:
1. Fill the tub with water from the hose. Let it sit in the sun for a couple hours to warm it up before the dog arrives. When the owner brings his or her pet, keep a plastic leash on the dog at all times.

2. Rinse the dog with the hose, keeping it at a low water power. Soap the animal up, according to the "Inside" directions in step 3.

3. Rinse carefully with a garden hose. Once the dog is out of the tub, it will want to shake itself. Since you're outside, let it shake, but don't let the dog off of the leash.

4. Finish drying the dog with a towel, and look at the "Inside" directions, step 6, for completing the job.

Study Partner

What You'll Need

Are you very good at math, science, reading, computer skills, or history? You might be able to use your expertise to help a younger student and earn cash as well.

- business kit
- pens
- pencils
- paper

(You will also need weekly lesson plans that can be provided by the student's parent or teacher.)

Get Prepared!

Let students and parents know about your offer by putting a notice on bulletin boards at school, in the local public library, and at your church or synagogue. Also, let your teachers know that you are available as a tutor.

Doing the Job

A few days before the tutoring session:

1. Work out a weekly schedule that is acceptable to everyone involved. Decide with the student's parent what is the best studying environment for the student. A few choices are at the student's house, at the public library, or even at your own house. The place will vary depending on what works best for each individual student. At this time, decide the length of each session, usually half an hour or an hour.

2. Sit down with the parent and student, and set realistic goals. For instance, if the youngster is getting D's in math, you may want to help him work his grade up to a C by midyear, and a B by the end of the year.

3. Thoroughly read the lesson that has been provided by the student's parent or teacher. Be sure to ask the teacher any questions you have, because the younger student will turn to you for answers. Write out your lesson plans and think of ways to add interest (for example, by using flash cards).

The tutoring session:

4. Begin with the more difficult material, saving the easier material for last. Review the main topic with the child. If you are working from a book, survey the lesson by reading the titles, subheadings, and any introductory or closing paragraphs out loud.

5. Now have your student read the material. Ask if there are any points that he or she doesn't understand. Ask questions about the main points to make sure he or she understands it.

6. If you find that the student is becoming frustrated, just talk for a while until he or she relaxes. Always be encouraging, patient, and positive.

7. Throughout the session look for the student's strong points, then finish the lesson by mentioning them.

Shopper's Special

What You'll Need

Are you well organized? Do you like to shop? There are plenty of holidays throughout the year, and plenty of things that need to be done to prepare for these holidays. Helping neighbors with their holiday shopping chores may be perfect for you, because you'll have fun and make money, too!

- business kit
- envelopes

- backpack
- fanny pack or wallet

(This list will vary, depending on the transportation you are using. If you are riding a bicycle, add baskets or saddlebags. If you are taking the bus, carry plenty of change for your fare. If you are walking, use a cart or wagon.)

Get Prepared!

Think about the services you will offer. You could shop for decorations, holiday foods, and gift wrap. You might also offer to go along with your client as a shopper's assistant. List all of these services on a flier, and distribute the fliers in your neighborhood.

Doing the Job

1. Visit your client, and write down any instructions in your notebook. Read them back to your client, and ask any questions you may have. Collect the amount of money you will need from your client, put it in an envelope, and mark the amount and the client's name on the front. Keep the envelope safe in an inside pocket of your jacket or in a fanny pack.

2. Every time you purchase an item, count your change on the spot to be sure it is correct. Put the change in the client's envelope.

3. Check everything against your list. When you deliver the items to your client, check your list with the client and give him or her any receipts and change.

Clowning Around

What You'll Need

Do you like to make people laugh? Are you a natural clown? Being a party clown and entertaining children may be the perfect job for you, and the money you can earn is no laughing matter.

- business kit
- costume
- makeup
- games or other activities
- balloons (optional)
- party favors (optional)

Get Prepared!

Have a friend or family member take pictures of you in your clown costume to show to prospective clients. Your costume does not need to be expensive. You can design your own costume with clothing from a secondhand store, or check out the sales right after Halloween. Most of all, you need to feel comfortable in the costume you put together.

Doing the Job

Two days before the party:

1. Be sure you have all the supplies that you plan to use, such as games, balloons, or inexpensive party favors such as party poppers (see page 68).

The day of the party:

2. Your client may want you to make a surprise entrance, so be prepared to arrive in costume.

3. There are plenty of ways to keep youngsters entertained. You can play games, tell jokes, perform magic tricks, or read silly stories. The most important thing is that everyone enjoys the party. If it's a birthday party, don't forget to do a special trick or give a silly gift to the birthday child!

Questions to Ask

What time should you arrive? How long will you be needed? How many children have been invited? How old are they? What's the occasion for the party? Is there a theme?

Cash for Trash

Collecting recyclables can be a very useful service. You can earn cash from clients for hauling away the trash, then get an extra bonus for redeeming the material.

What You'll Need

- business kit
- cart or wagon
- heavy gloves
- large plastic bags
- twine
- scissors

Get Prepared!

Use fliers to alert your neighbors to your service. Don't forget to leave fliers with local small businesses, too.

Doing the Job

1. Locate recycling centers in your area, and find out what their policies are. Most places will take newspapers, soda cans, and clear glass bottles. Some centers may also take plastics and more unusual items such as frozen food trays or pie plates.

2. Decide what types of material you will collect and how often you will pick up. Cans, glass, and newspapers may need to be picked up weekly, or even twice a week.

3. Set up a schedule with each client, and put this information in your calendar. You may schedule all of your pickups for the weekend, or service small areas on different days after school.

4. Once you have acquired your collections, you need to sort the material and prepare it for the recycling center. Cardboard boxes should be flattened and neatly stacked. With the twine, tie newspapers into small bundles each about a foot high. Some centers require that glass be separated into plain and colored glass.

5. It may be possible to handle visits to the recycling center with a wagon or cart. As your business grows, however, or if the recycling center isn't nearby, you may need to enlist the aid of someone with a car (a willing parent, perhaps).

Plenty of Paperwork

What You'll Need

Get Prepared!

Doing the Job

Small businesses are often loaded down with mountains of paperwork, such as filing and mailing. Many business owners would appreciate extra help, and you'll appreciate the extra money!

• business kit

A crisp, businesslike flier is the way to advertise this service. Small businesses and offices are likely targets for your efforts, but don't forget schools, clubs, and religious organizations.

1. Dress neatly and always arrive at the job on time. Listen carefully to the instructions, and write everything in your notebook that the client wants you to do. Then, look back over your notes to make sure you don't have any questions. By taking a moment to ask before you do something, you can avoid expensive, time-consuming mistakes.

2. When mailing letters, be sure that the name on the letter matches that on the envelope. Some companies may supply pre-addressed, stick-on labels; others may give you a list of addresses that need to be typed or handwritten on the envelopes.

3. When filing, pay close attention to detail and follow the instructions exactly. File papers neatly, and be sure they always face forward so that they can be read easily. When you are finished with the work, ask if there is anything else you can help with. A friendly and hardworking personality, along with clean, efficient work, often ensures repeat business for you!

Scrumptious Snacks!

What You'll Need

Get Prepared!

Doing the Job

If you have a special knack for baking in the kitchen, preparing and selling sweet snacks might be a good opportunity for you. This is a job that can help you earn extra money over your summer vacation.

- business kit
- large basket
- large checkered cloth
- food supplies
- plastic food wrap
- paper baking cups
- stick-on labels
- brown paper bags
- napkins
- fanny pack
- $5 in change

Since this is a food-oriented business, you should check with the local city hall to see whether you are required to have a special license, or whether there are any restrictions.

A few days before:

1. Decide what snacks you will offer for sale. Choose items that keep well for a while without being refrigerated, such as brownies, cupcakes, cookies, and fudge. You may want to offer fresh fruit as well, such as apples, oranges, or bananas. Or try putting together healthy snacks of nuts and raisins in several small plastic bags.

The day before:

2. Be sure that the area where you are working is clean, that you have all of your ingredients, and that all of the food items are fresh. (Just a reminder: Are you incorporating the cost of all the supplies into your fee? Look at the chart on page 4 if you need help!)

3. Completely clean the preparation area, and wash all utensils.

4. When the baked goods are cool, cut brownies into 2-inch squares or fudge into 1-inch squares. Put cupcakes into pretty paper baking cups and top with a thin layer of icing. Wrap each snack and label it. Wash, dry, and wrap any fruit.

The selling day:

5. Line your basket with a clean cloth, and pack the food so that nothing will be squashed. Tuck extra paper napkins and bags in one side to have ready in case you are asked for them.

6. Carry at least $5 worth of change in your fanny pack. Grab your basket of goodies, and head to the nearest park or local sports event. But always ask permission before you go onto private property.

$$$ **TIP:** To make money on this project, you need to sell your treats at least two or three days a week. You'll build up a steady clientele if you are reliable in your visits (for instance, visiting the park every other day at 2 P.M.).

Helping Hand

If you have a little time each day, or perhaps extra time on weekends, how about being a senior citizen's helper? In this job, you can make money and a special friend, too!

What You'll Need:

- business kit
- casual clothes

(The tools you will need for this service will probably change from day to day.)

Get Prepared!

Leave a business card or flier at the local senior citizen center, or at your church or synagogue. List on the flier the times you are available and the jobs that you could do.

Doing the Job

1. When you first meet a client, ask what types of jobs he or she needs done, and write these down in your notebook.

2. Your client may want you to do a variety of simple chores on a regular basis, such as light housekeeping, running errands, walking a pet, or taking out the trash.

3. You could bring along a book to read aloud, or offer to help with letter writing or other paperwork. You may even suggest an occasional stroll around the neighborhood. Some older people may simply enjoy having company.

Pool Profit

Although most swimming-pool owners love their pools, few like to clean them. Assisting homeowners on a weekly basis with this chore (or eventually learning to do it on your own) can leave you swimming in profits!

What You'll Need

- business kit
- clean rags

(The pool owner will have the equipment and supplies needed.)

Get Prepared!

Leave cards with neighbors who have pools. Ask for permission to leave fliers at stores that sell pool-cleaning supplies.

Doing the Job

1. If you are an assistant, leave the job of testing the water and adding chemicals to the owner. Carefully watch how this step is done and learn all you can, because the more you can do on your own, the more money people will pay for your service.

2. Use a long-handled skimmer to remove any floating leaves or insects on the surface of the water. With a soft brush, gently scrub the tile along the edge of the pool. Also gently scrub the steps in the shallow end and the ladder in the deep end to remove any dirt.

3. To remove leaves or dirt on the pool floor, vacuum the pool according to the owner's instructions. Begin at the shallow end and use a back-and-forth motion so that you cover the entire bottom.

4. The pool filter should also be checked and cleaned. If the owner wants you to do this, have him or her show you exactly how to do it.

5. When you are finished, wipe off the equipment with a clean rag, then put it all away.

Party Pal Planner

What You'll Need

Get Prepared!

Doing the Job

Today's busy parents don't always have time to prepare for a youngster's birthday, but that might provide just the job opportunity you are looking for. Many moms and dads would be grateful for the help of a party planner.

- business kit
- list of phone numbers and addresses of party shops, bakeries, stationers

This project is best advertised by word of mouth. Until you get your business off the ground, though, fliers are a good way to advertise. Note on the flier a list of services that you offer, such as shopping for party supplies, writing invitations, gift wrapping, party setup, and decorating. Dress neatly and deliver the fliers in person to neighbors who have small children.

Two weeks before the party:
1. Help the client with writing and mailing invitations.

One week before the party:
2. Order a cake if the client has requested it. Plan the games you would like to play. If you need any supplies or prizes, buy them now. Also pick up any decorations and supplies. Estimate the amount of cash you will need to cover these expenses, and ask your client for that amount. Keep any receipts so that you can give these to your client, along with the proper change.

The day before the party:
3. If you are offering gift wrapping, set aside time now to take care of this chore.

The day of the party:
4. Arrive at least two hours before the party begins so that you can put up the decorations and help the parents with any last-minute preparations.

5. During the party you can help organize games, keep track of who gave what gifts (so thank-you notes can be written later), and serve the cake.

6. When the party is over, expect to spend an extra thirty minutes to an hour to clear tables and countertops, wash dishes, put everything away, and take out the trash.

Questions to Ask

What sort of party is it? Is there a theme in mind? How many children will be invited? How old are they? How much money does the client want to spend on games, decorations, cake, and so on?

Ready for Rental

What You'll Need

ADULT SUPERVISION RECOMMENDED
Have you noticed many FOR RENT or FOR LEASE signs in your neighborhood? These signs can mean a business opportunity for you. The owners might be very interested in a cleanup service that "moves in" when the tenants move out.

- business kit
- large plastic bucket
- rubber gloves
- glass cleaner
- scouring powder
- paper towels

- clean rags
- soft bristle brush
- several sponges
- mop
- broom

(This list will vary, depending on the services you offer.)

Get Prepared!

This job is similar in some ways to "House Helper" (see page 21), but instead of homeowners, your customers are real-estate agents and apartment managers. Let them know about your service. Supply them with a list of the chores you do, such as oven cleaning, cleaning floors and windows, and papering cupboards.

Doing the Job

1. Begin with tough jobs such as oven cleaning, window washing, and bathroom scouring. For oven cleaning, always wear rubber gloves and follow the package directions on the cleaner exactly. You may need to get an adult to help you. Use nonabrasive cleaners when scrubbing bathtubs or sinks. See page 56 for tips on window washing.

2. Next, clean and dust all counters and shelves. If the rental property is furnished, be sure to dust and polish the surfaces of the furniture. Look for cobwebs behind furniture or in corners. Don't forget to dust any blinds. Clean mirrors with glass cleaner, then polish with a soft rag.

3. Now sweep and mop the floors, closets, and outside porches. If a vacuum cleaner is available, vacuum any carpets.

4. Finally, empty all trash containers. Leave your business card on the kitchen counter, with a couple of extras that can be passed along!

Literary Legwork

What You'll Need

You might be surprised to learn that a visit to your local library could be an opportunity to earn cash. If you are well organized, you could provide a library service for your friends and neighbors.

- business kit
- backpack

Get Prepared!

First, check with your library to be sure that you can use your customer's library card. The library might ask for written permission from the card holder. To reach your customers, distribute fliers throughout your neighborhood. On the flier, list the services you offer, including obtaining books, audiotapes, or videos, and making copies of material.

Doing the Job

1. Stop at your client's home to find out what he or she needs. If you will be checking out material, note the title and author. If you are to make copies, ask for change to run the copy machine. Don't forget to get the client's library card.

2. At the library, check each item off your list as you find it. If an item you want is checked out, make a note of the date that it is supposed to be returned. If you make copies, label each copy with the book or magazine that it came from. Note the number and cost of the copies on a piece of paper to give to your customer as a receipt.

3. When you are combining errands for many people, slip a piece of paper with each client's name into the books or tape containers.

4. Using the list of items you checked out, keep track of the due dates. Call your customer two or three days before the books are due to remind them that you will be picking them up, and arrange a time to pick up the items. When you return materials, check them off in your notebook. Keep a record of returns in case there is any question in the future.

CLIENT	ADDRESS	BOOKS	DUE DATE	RETURNED
MR. ANDREW CLAY	1126 BROXTON HEIGHTS	"WOMEN WHO RUN WITH THE DOPES"	6/16	✓
MR. I.M. MENDICANT	235 PENURY RD.	"HOW TO MAKE A MILLION IN 7 DAYS"	7/1	✓
MR. WILLIAM R. CYRUS	13789 NASHVILLE STREET	"SONGWRITING MADE E-Z"	7/3	
MRS. SMITH	4900 CROCKER AVE.	"PERFECT PIE-CRUST"		
MS. BAMBI LOCKLEER	333 HOLLYWOOD WAY	"ACTING WORKS"		

Wrap It Up

What You'll Need

When busy adults are preparing for a birthday party or for holidays, they may be very pleased to enlist the help of a wrapping service.

- business kit
- boxes
- ribbons and bows
- scissors
- wrapping paper
- tissue
- tape
- removable self-stick notes

Get Prepared!

Show photographs of sample packages that you have made and several samples of wrapping paper. You want to show off your creativity, so use your imagination. For example, for a comic hero buff, wrap a gift in the Sunday funnies. Or, use a diaper and diaper pins to wrap a baby shower gift.

Doing the Job

1. If possible, go to your client's house to do the actual wrapping. This makes it easier for you, because you won't have to carry around a load of packages. However, this also means you need to be very organized and bring all wrapping, bows, and any other accessories with you. Before wrapping the gifts, meet with the client to find out exactly how he or she would like the gifts decorated.

2. When you are ready to begin wrapping, remove any price tags. On a small self-stick note write what the gift is.

3. If you are wrapping a breakable object, pack the box carefully with extra tissue to cushion the item. For clothing, line the box with two or three sheets of tissue.

4. To wrap a standard package, place the box in the center of a piece of paper cut to a suitable size.

5. Bring sides #1 and #2 together over the package so that they overlap slightly, and tape them securely.

6. Trim extra paper off the sides, leaving just enough to cover the ends of the package. Then fold in side #3 to point B and side #4 to point C.

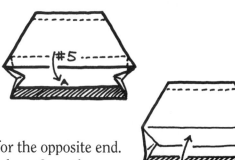

7. Fold in side #5 to point A and tape it down, and finally take side #6 and fold it over side #5. Try to keep the paper as unwrinkled and flat as possible.

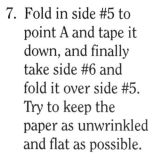

8. Repeat steps 6 and 7 for the opposite end. Add a pretty ribbon or bow. Once the package is wrapped, immediately put the self-stick note on the gift so you don't forget what you wrapped!

Walking Partner

What You'll Need

Get Prepared!

Doing the Job

There are plenty of people who would like to start an exercise program but just can't seem to get going, or don't want to exercise alone. You can help get them on the "right track" and make some money, too, by being a walking partner.

- business kit
- comfortable walking shoes
- watch

Advertise this service by getting permission to put up fliers at stores where walking shoes are sold, at senior citizen centers, and at the bulletin board at the local high school track.

1. Offer your client a choice of places to walk, such as the high school track, a local park, or around the client's neighborhood. In some areas people have even taken up walking for exercise in indoor shopping malls!

2. It is your job to motivate your client to exercise. You need to be as flexible as possible and be available for those folks who prefer early morning walks, as well as those who prefer walking later in the day. Work out a time that is good for both of you, then always call a little ahead of time to make sure your exercise buddy will be at your exercise spot.

3. Note the time when you begin, and keep up a steady pace throughout the walk. If the client is just starting to exercise, keep the pace slow and the walk down to fifteen or twenty minutes, two or three times a week. Your client can increase the distance and pace when he or she is ready.

Kiddy Kare Roundup

What You'll Need

This is a special twist on baby-sitting. If you are good with young children, you could offer to baby-sit for small groups of three or four children during weddings, meetings, classes, or adults' parties. This is a perfect business for a partnership!

- business kit
- stick-on name tags
- books
- games
- colored paper and markers
- other craft material

Get Prepared!

Take a batch of fliers to the local supermarket and leave them under the windshield wipers of cars (especially those with children's car seats in them!) in the parking lot. Ask permission to leave or hang fliers at party supply stores, as well as local churches and synagogues. On your flier, include the age range of children you feel comfortable handling.

Doing the Job

1. Arrive at least thirty minutes before the children are due, and set up the area with any craft supplies you've brought.

2. As the youngsters arrive, make a name tag for each child. Ask parents whether they have any special instructions, and write these down in your notebook.

3. Your job is to keep the children entertained, safe, and reasonably quiet while their parents are busy. There are plenty of things you can do, such as play games or color. You might read stories or even make up a story together.

4. When the parents have returned for their children, be sure that the area is clean. Never let a child leave with someone other than his or her parent, unless this has already been arranged with the parents.

> **$$$ TIP:** Your hourly fee should be based on how many children you will be caring for. For example, you could charge $2 per hour for each child.

 # It Pays to Advertise

What You'll Need

Get Prepared!

Doing the Job

Advertising is a key to success in many businesses. One way that businesses advertise is by sending out fliers to potential customers. If you have time and energy, delivering those fliers can be a successful business of its own.

- business kit
- sturdy walking shoes

When you see fliers in your neighborhood, check to see who the advertiser is, and pay them a visit. You can also approach local business owners to tell them about your service, and don't forget to leave your business card.

1. Ask your clients where they want the fliers distributed, and whether they want the fliers to be passed out to individuals, left door to door, or placed under car windshield wipers.

2. Be sure to let an adult know your route and how long you'll be gone. You may want to take along a friend to help (of course, that also means sharing the profits).

3. Be sure all the fliers are distributed. On a windy day, tuck them in or under something so that they will not blow away (or get wet on a rainy day).

THINK SAFETY! If you are leaving fliers door to door, never accept a stranger's invitation to step inside the house or apartment. Also, this is a job that should be done only during daylight hours.

Moving Day

What You'll Need

Get Prepared!

Doing the Job

A "sold" sign on a home in your neighborhood may be a sign of opportunity for you. Help people who are moving out of their home by packing their belongings.

- business kit
- gloves

Let local real-estate agents and apartment managers know about your service. Give them some business cards, and ask them if they could recommend you to people who are planning a move.

1. Before you arrive, make sure the client understands that he or she is responsible for providing boxes, packing tape, and newspaper or bubble wrap. Your job is to make sure that the contents of each box arrive at their destination safely. Check to see that each box is sturdy.

2. Pack similar items together. For example, pack clothing in one box and breakable items in another. Also, remember that some-one will have to lift what you are packing, so don't make any one box too heavy.

3. When packing breakable items, first wrap them in newspaper or bubble wrap, then place them carefully in the box. Pad additional paper around each item.

4. When the packing box is full, tape it shut and label it as descrip-tively as you can, according to the type of items inside. You may also want to label the room each box should go in.

 # Let the Sun Shine In

What You'll Need

Get Prepared!

Doing the Job

ADULT SUPERVISION RECOMMENDED

Although everyone likes having sparkling clean windows, most homeowners dread cleaning them. This gives you a chance to really "clean up"!

- business kit
- vinegar and water
- sponge
- large towel or old sheet
- spray bottle
- bucket
- rubber gloves
- soft rags
- paper towels
- squeegee
- step stool or small ladder (optional)

The best time to start this business is in the spring. You may also find new customers at holiday times when people are preparing their homes to entertain family and guests. Begin by paying a visit to your neighbors. Tell them about your service, and leave a business card with your name and telephone number. Drop your business card by local small businesses as well.

Inside:

1. To prevent drips, place an old towel or sheet on the floor under the window you are about to wash. Put the rubber gloves on.

2. You can mix your own cleaning solution by mixing one part vinegar to two parts water. Then pour the liquid into an empty spray bottle.

3. For some of the windows you may need a small step stool, but you still may need an adult to help you reach the top corners of the windows. Lightly spray the solution onto the glass. Use a paper towel or rag to clean the glass.

4. Complete the job by polishing the window with a dry, soft rag.

Outside:

1. This is often a dirtier chore than cleaning the insides of windows, so you may want to charge more. For a particularly tough job, begin by mixing some cleaning solution in a bucket.

2. You may need a small step stool to reach the dirty top corners, but make sure the stool is on level ground. Use a sponge to rinse the glass. Then, instead of using a paper towel or rag, use a squeegee to remove the solution.

3. Finally, polish the window with a dry, soft rag.

Something More

If you are artistic, you might add window decorating to your list of services. For birthdays or for holidays such as Valentine's Day, Halloween, or Christmas, you can use simple construction-paper cutouts, ribbon, cardboard figures, stencils and spray-on "snow," or other supplies to dress up a home's windows for the festivities. Check your local library for books with window decorating ideas. Be sure to photograph your creations to show prospective clients.

'Tis the Season

What You'll Need

Get Prepared!

Doing the Job

If you live in snow country, you can earn cold cash in winter by shoveling snow from walks and driveways.

- business kit
- warm gloves
- waterproof boots

- snow shovel
- hand-held ice scraper

Listen to the weather reports. When snow is predicted, leave business cards or fliers with neighbors, explaining your service. Don't forget to check with the owners of small businesses, who may appreciate having their sidewalks cleared after a storm.

1. Dress warmly, with layers of clothing that can be removed if you feel overheated. Wear waterproof boots with nonskid soles.

2. For wide driveways, begin in the center and work outward. Sometimes the entire drive needn't be cleared—only enough so that the garage can be opened and the car pulled in and out. Pile snow where it won't become an obstacle to anything else (such as the mailbox or the front door).

3. Once you've cleared the snow, chip away any slippery patches of ice with the ice scraper, particularly from any steps.

$$\text{---}$$

\$\$\$ TIP: Some people like to have sand or salt spread on slippery walkways. If your client requests it, cover your costs by charging a little extra for providing this service.

Both materials have their pros and cons. Salt helps to melt ice, but it can burn lawns, rust cars, and irritate the feet of animals. Sand provides good footing and is harmless to plants and animals, but it is messy. If you use either, use it sparingly.

Neat and Trim

Mother Nature provides special job opportunities in autumn. Raking leaves from flower beds and lawns is a task that many homeowners will happily pay to have done.

What You'll Need

- business kit
- sturdy gloves
- rake
- long-handled garden broom
- plastic trash bags

Get Prepared!

Check around your neighborhood for homes with plenty of trees on the property. Leave a flier or business card on their doorsteps, describing your service.

Doing the Job

1. Divide the yard into sections. Work in one area at a time, raking the leaves from each section into a pile.

2. Bag each pile before moving on to the next section. This way a sudden wind won't undo all of your hard work.

3. Gently rake leaves from flower gardens, being careful not to injure the plants.

4. Find out how your customer wants you to dispose of the leaves. Some people like to put a thick layer of leaves around flower gardens to protect the plants in winter. Finally, sweep the driveways and the walkways.

Painter's Assistant

After a few years of wear and tear, a home can look dull and drab. Many homeowners are choosing to perk things up themselves with a fresh coat of paint. A good assistant can make a tremendous chore such as painting a house simpler and less tiring. If you do this job well, you may find your services in demand.

What You'll Need

- business kit
- plenty of rags
- masking tape
- hammer

- screwdriver
- paint scraper
- glass scraper
- bucket

- rubber gloves (optional)
- lightweight goggles

(The client should supply plaster, paint, brushes, rollers, drop cloths, cleaners, and sandpaper.)

Get Prepared!

Make a list of the jobs you can do, such as mixing paint, scraping, light sanding, patching nail holes, washing walls, taping windows, and cleaning up spills and equipment. The more things you know how to do, the more marketable you are. If you want to learn how to do any of the above, ask a parent or a painter you know, or call a paint supply store for information. Place your fliers or business cards on bulletin boards at the market, at paint stores, or anywhere home-improvement products are sold.

Doing the Job

1. As an assistant, it is your job to help the painter and make sure the painting job goes smoothly. When you are given a chore, listen to the instructions and follow them carefully. If something is unclear, don't be afraid to ask questions.

2. Take a little extra time to tape glass or cover furniture correctly, rather than spending time to clean up a mess later. Find ways to prevent work from piling up. Clean equipment as you finish with it, and remove empty paint cans, old nails, soiled rags, and any trash. Clean up spills as soon as they happen.

3. When the job is finished, be sure that partially filled paint cans are closed securely. Carefully remove all tape and coverings, and scrape off any excess dried paint from all window glass.

4. Wash out buckets and fold drop cloths. Collect all tools and supplies in one area. The materials you need for cleaning brushes (soap and water, mineral spirits, and so on) will depend on the type of paint that was used. Follow the instructions on the paint can. If you aren't sure, call the store and ask for the safest way to handle it. The client should pay for the cleaning supplies.

THINK SAFETY! Be "Earth safe." Never wash or rinse any type of paint into water that will flow into street gutters and pollute water supplies.

Employment Agency

What happens if your service business (such as baby-sitting, pet walking, or lawn mowing) is doing so well that you have more work than you can handle? If you are dependable and well-organized, this could be an extra opportunity to make money!

What You'll Need

- business kit
- two notebooks

Get Prepared!

You need two lists of clients: customers who need to have a job done, and kids looking for jobs to do. To reach the customers, put up fliers at markets and senior citizen centers. To reach prospective employees, ask among your friends and fellow students.

Doing the Job

1. In your "resource" notebook make a list of *reliable* kids who want to make a little cash. List the kids' skills (lawn mowing, for example) and experience, as well as their phone numbers.

2. When a customer calls to have a job done, take down the information in a second notebook, including the type of job it is, when it must be done, and how much it will pay. Find someone from your resource book who is available and able to do the job.

3. On the calendar from your business kit, record the date that each job is to be done, and call the employee the day before to be sure he or she will be on time.

4. After the job is done, call the customer to be sure he or she is satisfied. Make a note of whether the customer would use the same worker again. Collect your fee from the youngster who did the job.

$$$ TIP: Your fee for this service is a percentage of the amount paid to the person who did the work. Ten percent is reasonable. You earn your fees by keeping an updated list of clients and by carefully matching the clients and workers. If the clients are not happy with the workers you choose, they will look for their own workers elsewhere.

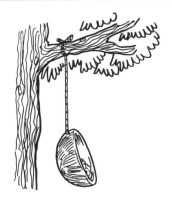

Craft Corner

The next 10 ways to earn money rely on the creative and artistic abilities in everyone. Each project is a fun, unique craft that you can make and sell to eager buyers. If you enjoy designing and selling homemade crafts, one or several of the following might be just the profit-maker for you!

Unless otherwise stated, the following projects give you instructions for making one craft. However, to earn money on any of the projects, you will need to make (and sell!) several. Refer back to page 4 to help you figure out costs and prices.

Terrific Tees

What You'll Need

PARENTAL SUPERVISION RECOMMENDED

Everyone loves T-shirts! With this project you could create custom tees for such special events as birthdays, anniversaries, holidays, or even sporting events.

- business kit
- order forms
- paper
- markers
- dye
- sequins
- needle and thread
- iron

- puff paint
- T-shirts (customers may wish to supply their own)
- small plastic margarine containers
- pencil
- washing machine and dryer

- scissors
- large piece of thick cardboard
- rubber gloves
- rags
- paintbrushes
- newspaper

Get Prepared!

Why not make and wear one of your specially designed T-shirts as an ad for your business? When someone tells you what a great T-shirt you're wearing, pull out an order form and you're in business! If your shirts are unique and your business seems to be growing, try making a deal with a local store owner to sell your work for a percentage of sales.

Doing the Job

1. You can decorate T-shirts by sewing on sequins, and by using puff paints and dyes. Check craft books and stores for other methods, and choose the one that you feel most comfortable with.

2. Show your client a few samples of your best designs. You can either put these designs on shirts or draw them on sheets of paper. Find out whether the shirt is for a holiday or special event. For example, you could design a shirt and add a name and date on it for an anniversary or birthday. For a sporting event, you could prepare tie-dyed shirts in the school's colors.

3. Draw up an order form listing the client's name as well as the size of the shirt, the type of design, and the day that it is due. Give a copy to the client.

4. When you are ready to begin working on your product, pre-wash the T-shirt, following the instructions on the label.

5. Spread newspapers on a large table or countertop, then prepare small amounts (about a cup each) of the two or three dyes that you are going to use. Put them in separate plastic margarine containers. Follow the package directions. While the T-shirt is washing, practice your dyeing technique and design on rags.

6. Once the T-shirt is dry, cut a large piece of cardboard to fit inside the T-shirt. Slip the cardboard cutout inside the T-shirt to prevent the dye from coloring the back of the shirt, then lightly sketch your design on the shirt in pencil.

7. Paint in your design with dye, using a different brush for each color. It's a good idea to wear rubber gloves to protect your hands from the dye.

8. Once the shirt is dry, turn it inside out. With a parent's help, iron the fabric with a warm iron to keep the colors from running when you wash it.

9. Use puff paints to write names or phrases, and sew on sequins to dress up the T-shirt. Be creative!

$$$ TIP: You can expand your business to include other items such as book bags, purses, sneakers, or notebooks.

For the Birds

What You'll Need

Get Prepared!

Doing the Job

PARENTAL SUPERVISION REQUIRED

Many animal lovers have a warm place in their hearts for wild birds. Selling filled bird feeders is a great way to earn money and give Mother Nature a helping hand, too!

- business kit
- coconut
- mixing bowl
- pan
- wooden spoon
- saw

- small drill
- plastic wrap
- heavy cord
- bread crumbs
- 1 cup suet (a kind of fat)
- saucepan

- ½ cup raisins
- peanuts
- grater
- knife
- guide to local birds (optional)

If you do your homework, this can be a year-round business, because the types of birds that live in your neighborhood may change with the seasons. Find out what birds are found in your area and at what time of year, and what sort of food will attract those birds. Using this information, develop product lines for spring/summer and fall/winter. Below, you will find directions for making two coconut-shell feeders filled with peanut-coconut birdcake. Check your library for other ideas.

1. Ask an adult to help you to saw the husk of a coconut in half and scrape out the meat. Set the meat aside.

2. With a parent's help, drill a small hole near the open edge of each half. For each half, fit a 12-inch length of cord through the hole, then tie a large knot in the end inside

DRILL A HOLE IN SHELL AND THREAD CORD THROUGH...

...THEN TIE A LARGE KNOT ON THE END OF THE CORD.

the shell. Tie a loop in the other end of the cord so that each feeder can be hung from a branch. Set the feeders aside.

3. Now you're ready to make the food for your feathered friends. Melt the suet in a saucepan over low heat. Meanwhile, chop the raisins and peanuts, then place them in a large mixing bowl.

4. Take the coconut meat that was inside the coconut, and grate it. Add the coconut and the bread crumbs to the large mixing bowl.

5. Add the melted suet and mix well. Let it cool, then fill the feeders with the birdcake mixture. Cover each feeder with plastic wrap for delivery.

Party Poppers!

Holidays present a wonderful opportunity for the young business-person who can design and make items to help celebrate such special days as Valentine's Day, Halloween, Thanksgiving, and Christmas or Hanukkah. The filling you choose will depend on the holiday. These fun party favors can start your business with a bang and bring added surprise to any holiday celebration.

What You'll Need

- business kit
- scissors
- colorful tissue paper
- ruler
- pencil

- white glue
- confetti
- thin, brightly colored ribbon

- small wrapped candies
- cardboard tube from a roll of bathroom tissue

Get Prepared!

Make a few sample favors to show your customers. Print your business name and telephone number on each. Display the samples in a decorated box or basket that you can carry as you visit possible customers in your neighborhood. Be ready to take orders, but be sure that you can deliver all of them on time.

Doing the Job

1. Cut a sheet of colored tissue into a rectangle about 10 inches by 12 inches. Cut the cardboard tube from a roll of bathroom tissue in half across the middle.

2. Place the colored-tissue rectangle on a tabletop so that the 10-inch length is at the bottom. Put the two cardboard tube halves together at the bottom of the tissue. Glue the edge of the tissue paper around the tube so that the paper will stay in place, then roll up the tube in the tissue.

3. Carefully tie one side of the tube closed with ribbon. Tie it tightly, but be careful not to rip the tissue paper.

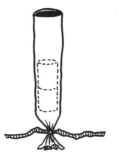

4. Depending on the holiday, fill the tube with fun goodies. If it's New Year's Eve, you may want to fill the tube with confetti and a few wrapped candies. For Valentine's Day, fill them with chocolate kisses. And for the Fourth of July, put red, white, and blue jelly-beans in the tube. Once you've filled the tube with treats, tie the open end closed.

5. To get the goodies, hold the tube with both hands and break it open. It'll burst open with a pop, and some yummy treats will spill out.

$$\$\$\$$ TIP: Try to sell your party poppers in groups of 10, 12, or even 20. You can plan ahead by doing steps 1 through 3 ahead of time, then when you get a large order, just fill up the tubes and you're done!

Sweet Scents

What You'll Need

Get Prepared!

Doing the Job

The aroma of fruit and spice is a special treat in fall and winter. Making scented pomanders of oranges and cloves is a good way to spread this special variety of holiday cheer.

- business kit
- large orange or apple
- knitting needle

- one box of whole cloves
- clean cloth
- 12 inches of red or green ribbon

Pomanders are easiest to sell if you prepare samples, visit your neighbors, and take orders. As the holiday season nears, you might be able to find local art fairs or other events where you can sell these pleasant-smelling decorations.

1. In order for your pomander to develop properly by delivery time, you must start about one month ahead. Use the knitting needle to punch shallow, equally spaced holes (a little more than $\frac{1}{8}$ inch apart) in the skin of an orange or apple.

2. Push the point of a clove into each hole until all are filled. Now place the clove-studded fruit on a piece of clean cloth in a warm, very dry place (a closet works well).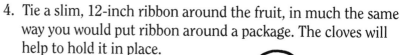

3. Check the fruit every few days to see that it is drying properly. It should shrivel and be fully dried within about four weeks.

4. Tie a slim, 12-inch ribbon around the fruit, in much the same way you would put ribbon around a package. The cloves will help to hold it in place.

5. Knot the ribbon at the top of the fruit, then tie the ends together to form a loop for hanging the pomander. It is ideal to hang in the kitchen or around a doorknob in any room.

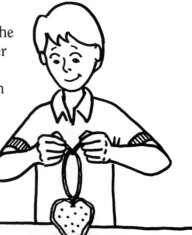

Fancy Fans

What You'll Need

Decorative fans are easy to make, and they look lovely hanging on a wall or used as a centerpiece. This is a craft that can quickly be turned into cash.

- business kit
- pieces of cotton fabric or lace, each approximately 4 inches by 10 inches
- rubber tub or basin

- liquid starch
- rubber gloves
- aluminum foil
- ribbons, tassles, glitter, sequins

Get Prepared!

Doing the Job

You can sell your work in your neighborhood or ask local store owners to display your fans for a percentage of sales. You could make your business cards on small paper fans that you fold!

1. Trim the edges of the fabric you have chosen so that it is even and there are no loose threads.

2. Wearing rubber gloves, pour liquid starch into the tub, about ½ inch deep. Soak the piece of fabric in the starch, then remove it and hold the fabric above the tub until it stops dripping.

3. Place the damp fabric on a piece of foil. Starting from the long end, fold up a 1-inch-wide strip. Turn the fabric over (along with the foil), and repeat this step. Continue to turn the fabric and fold until you have used all of the material.

4. Fold the foil over the fabric, and place a book on top of it to help the fan keep its shape.

5. Allow the fabric to dry overnight, then remove it from the foil. Hold the fan closed at one end and fan the other end open. Tie the closed end with ribbon. Decorate the fan with ribbon, tassles, glitter, sequins, or anything you like (or that your client has requested!).

Natural Wonders

What You'll Need

Get Prepared!

Doing the Job

While walking in the woods or in a park, you can turn items you collect into holiday cash. With a little imagination, wild mistletoe or fallen pinecones can become fast-selling holiday decorations.

- business kit
- mistletoe
- scissors
- pinecones
- 3-by-5-inch note cards

- red and green ribbon
- green or red thumbtacks
- glitter
- glue (preferably, that dries clear)
- newspaper

Prepare samples, display them to your neighbors, and take orders. To reach more people, ask your friends to go around their neighborhoods with samples. You can also ask local store owners to display your work for a percentage of sales.

Mistletoe:

1. Common mistletoe is a green plant with small white berries. It grows in the branches of trees, such as red maple and elm. If you live in an area where mistletoe is found, you can gather it yourself. If not, you can usually buy it from nurseries or Christmas tree growers.

2. Clip two or three 5-inch-long sprigs. Tie the sprigs together with red ribbon, and make a loop at the top. You may want to add a tiny jingle bell.

3. Sell the decorated sprigs for people to hang over doorways during the holiday season. (Along with your product, give each person a 3-by-5-inch note card that says mistletoe can be very harmful if eaten, so they need to keep it away from pets and small children.)

Pinecone decorations:

1. Making a wall or door decoration with three pinecones is easy. Begin by spreading newspaper on your worktable.

2. Paint a thin strip of glue along the open edges of each cone. Sprinkle the wet glue with glitter, then allow the cones to dry for about thirty minutes.

3. Cut three 12-inch-long strips of thin green or red ribbon, and tie each separately into three big loops. Center each loop on top of the pinecone and stick a thumbtack in it.

4. Gather together the three loose ends and hang from a nail, a doorknob, or a hook.

Fire Starters

What You'll Need

PARENTAL SUPERVISION REQUIRED
Most people love a crackling fire on a chilly winter evening. Sometimes getting that fire started, however, isn't so easy. You can make and sell a unique fire starter that is perfect for the job.

- business kit
- mini muffin tin
- old candles or candle wax
- wicks
- scissors
- double boiler or coffee can and pan
- tongs
- cooking mitt
- candy thermometer
- plastic wrap
- waxed paper
- long, slender pinecones (for example, blue spruce)
- various colored ribbons

Get Prepared!

Make a basket of free samples to pass out to your neighbors. Fliers can also be helpful with drawings of your items and a price list. Ask local store owners to display your work for a percentage of sales.

Doing the Job

1. With an adult's help, begin melting the old candles or candle wax slowly in the top of a double boiler or in a coffee can centered in a pan of heated water, until you have about 3 inches of wax. This step must be handled with care, because candle wax catches fire easily. A candy thermometer also comes in handy for checking that the wax is at the correct temperature (about 160 degrees Fahrenheit) and does not become too hot. If you are using old candles, use tongs to remove any bits of wick once the wax has melted.

2. Spread several sheets of waxed paper on your worktable. Protecting your hand with a cooking mitt, use tongs to dip each pinecone in the melted wax. Give the cone a light coating of wax (it isn't necessary to cover every bit), and lay it on its side on the waxed paper to dry.

3. Once the cones are covered, pour the remaining wax into the cups of a mini muffin tin. Cut as many 2-inch lengths of wick as you need, and quickly place them in each cup, leaving about ½ inch of wick extending from the edge of the wax.

4. Stand each cooled pinecone, wide end down, in each wax-filled cup. Be sure that some of the wick is sticking out from the side so that it can be lit later, then allow the wax to cool completely for at least an hour.

5. Place the tin in the freezer for about ten minutes. Then take it out of the freezer, and tip the tin so that the cones will slip out.

6. Wrap your fire starters individually in plastic wrap, and tie them with festive ribbons.

$$$ **TIP:** You might offer to sell the starters either singly or in decorative baskets or boxes that hold several.

Mantel Magic

What You'll Need

Get Prepared!

Doing the Job

PARENTAL SUPERVISION RECOMMENDED

The Christmas season offers some special opportunities to make money. If you can sew, you can make holiday cash and have fun, too, by designing and making cheerful stockings for families to hang from their mantels.

- business kit
- pencil
- scissors
- heavy red or green felt

- sewing needle
- heavy thread
- white glue
- lace
- bells

- sequins
- yarn
- lightweight cardboard

Prepare several different samples to show your customers. Fill a basket with stockings and sample materials and trims. Visit your neighbors and take orders several weeks ahead of time so you will have plenty of time to fill the orders.

1. On a sheet of lightweight cardboard, draw the outline of your stocking. (An average size would be approximately 24 inches long and 8 inches wide at the "ankle," but you may want to offer a variety of sizes.) Cut out the stocking pattern.

2. Place the pattern on the fabric you have chosen, and draw an outline of the stocking. Repeat so that you have two drawings. Cut out the stocking outlines from the fabric so that you have two pieces.

3. You may want to get a parent or an older sibling to help you with this next step. Securely stitch the two pieces together along the edges and around the foot, but leave the top open. When the stitching is complete, turn the stocking inside out.

4. Fold down the top to create a trim 3 or 4 inches long. Sew a loop of fabric or yarn to the top of the stocking on the "heel" side. This loop must be strong, because it will be used to hang the stocking. Decorate the trim with furry fabric, lace, bells, glitter, or whatever you choose. Be creative!

Candle Crafts

What You'll Need

PARENTAL SUPERVISION REQUIRED

Candles can be used for many occasions, including Christmas, Hanukkah, New Year's Eve, and even Valentine's Day. With practice and a little imagination, you can come up with designs that will guarantee income throughout the year.

- business kit
- old candles for wax
- old crayons for color
- gloves
- tongs
- candy thermometer

- deep double boiler or coffee can and pan
- long strips of wick
- decorations to press into the candles (optional)

(You can also get candle-making kits, dyes, wicks, and other supplies at most craft stores.)

Get Prepared!

While you are practicing your craft, photograph those candles you like the most. Bring your photo book and two or three candle samples when you visit potential customers. Art fairs and local specialty stores are also good places to show off your wares.

Doing the Job

1. With an adult's help, melt the wax slowly in a double boiler or in a coffee can centered in a pan of heated water, until you have about 6 inches of wax. If you wish to add color, drop in the color of crayons that you want. This step must be handled with care, because candle wax catches fire easily. A candy thermometer also comes in handy for checking that the wax is at the correct temperature (about 160 degrees Fahrenheit) and does not become too hot.

2. For standard, dipped candles, cut several 16-inch strips of candle wick. Fold each wick in half, and hold it in the center so that the two strings do not touch.

3. Dip the wicks as deeply as possible into the melted wax for one minute. Then lift them up, allowing any wax to drip back into the boiler (or can). Repeat this step over and over until the candles are as thick as you want them to be.

4. Once the candles have stopped dripping, hang them over a hook or nail until they are dry (at least three or four hours).

5. If you want to add decorations (for example, seashells), wait fifteen minutes or so until the wax is warm but firm, then press the decorations into the wax.

6. Finish your creation by cutting the wick to separate the two candles, then trimming each remaining wick to about ½ inch in length.

7. Sell your candles in groups of two, four, or even by the dozen!

50 Happy Birthday Wreath

Wreaths aren't just for Christmas anymore! More and more people are hanging wreaths for other holidays, too, just to add a festive decoration to the front door at any time of year. What could be a better way to celebrate a birthday than with a special wreath!

What You'll Need

- business kit
- Styrofoam wreath base
- colored tissue
- white glue
- thin florist's wire
- clippers
- ribbon
- bows
- paper streamers
- paper birthday party favors
- florist's tape
- newspaper

Get Prepared!

Make a sample wreath to show to friends and neighbors. Take orders at least three or four weeks in advance so that you have plenty of time to fill them. Don't forget to advertise by decorating your own front door, too!

Doing the Job

1. Cover your working surface with newspaper, and lay out all of your supplies.

2. Decide where the top of the wreath will be, and run a 12-inch strand of wire around it. Twist the ends of the wire together to keep it from coming undone. Wrap a smaller piece of wire around the first wrapped wire to form a loop for hanging.

FRONT

3. Lay a colorful piece of paper across the front of the Styrofoam, completly covering it. Poke a hole through the center of the paper, and wrap the tissue through the center and around the edge. Glue the tissue ends to the back of the wreath base, leaving the wire loop exposed.

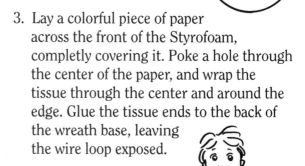

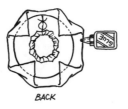

BACK

4. Turn it back to the front, and glue on birthday bows, colored paper streamers, and inexpensive plastic or paper party favors. Cover the entire wreath, being sure to cover any glue spots.